Asa and the Opals

Praise for Storyshares

"One of the brightest innovators and game-changers in the education industry."
– Forbes

"Your success in applying research-validated practices to promote literacy serves as a valuable model for other organizations seeking to create evidence-based literacy programs."
- Library of Congress

"We need powerful social and educational innovation, and Storyshares is breaking new ground. The organization addresses critical problems facing our students and teachers. I am excited about the strategies it brings to the collective work of making sure every student has an equal chance in life."
– Teach For America

"It's the perfect idea. There's really nothing like this. I mean, wow, this will be a wonderful experience for young people."
- Andrea Davis Pinkney, Executive Director, Scholastic

"Reading for meaning opens opportunities for a lifetime of learning. Providing emerging readers with engaging texts that are designed to offer both challenges and support for each individual will improve their lives for years to come. Storyshares is a wonderful start."
- David Rose, Co-founder of CAST & UDL

Asa and the Opals

Morgan Humphrey

Storyshares

Story Share, Inc.

24 N. Bryn Mawr Avenue #34C

Bryn Mawr, PA 19010-3304

www.storyshares.org

Inspiring reading with a new kind of book.

Interest Level: Middle School

Grade Level Equivalent: 5.5

9781642612875

Book design by Storyshares

Storyshares Presents

Chapter One

"CONFLICTS AMONG FAIRIES BEGAN long before the present day. However, they were kept in check by two powerful rulers: the Emperor Horticulturist Machalepi II and the Empress Horticulturist Saffron XXVI. These rulers were strong until the Battle of Cereus. Then they were overthrown and forced to retreat into hiding.

"The riots started over lack of food during an intense drought. Neither Machalepi II nor Saffron XXVI had any idea how to help the people. So, they simply gave what they had to those who needed it. This was highly effective until the Horticulturists ran out of supplies to give. The desperate, hungry public stormed the castle and took everything. The Horticulturists were forced to flee with only the clothes on their backs and their young daughter, Epazote III.

"Epazote III grew up in poverty. However, she received the same education as the future Empress Horticulturist. She did not see the world the same way as her parents did. Instead of seeing only the current starvation, she saw ways to stop it. Her parents would not allow her to try and regain the family's former power. But when her mother died of the contagious Fire Blight disease and her father went to serve in a local militia, she was left to decide her own future. She chose a path that would make her the most famous fairy leader in all of history.

"Epazote III boldly walked into a raging battle, the Battle of Snake's Head Fritillary. She declared that she had solved the problem of the drought. There were many doubts. Epazote III quickly proved herself by watering the ground with the blood of her first challenger and planting a tree in the newly softened earth.

"All enemies were imprisoned as she took back power. Food was restricted and water was not given to fairies but to plants. Riots became less frequent as Epazote III forced the people to see how serious she was about fixing the planet. She mastered the four elements: fire, earth, water, and air. She used these abilities to help the plants grow and end the drought. As the drought went away, so did the restrictions. By the end of Epazote III's reign, every fairy had food and water, and the plants were flourishing. Her people were dismayed when a tree fell on her, killing her and leaving her throne open.

"Luckily, she had trained four counselors before her death, and they took the throne. They were not only important because they made rules and enforced them. They also guarded the four elements: fire, earth, water, and air. The opal stones that held the power of the elements were kept safe in the Cereus Palace."

Chapter Two

ASAFETIDA FINISHED HER STORY and looked at the younglings below her. There were only three, and they were far too small to do any gardening. Still, it was her job to educate them on the fairy history. She also taught them how to carry on the Empress Horticulturist's legacy to protect the planet. In a year or so, the younglings would be big enough to begin working.

"Miss Asa," said Jessamine, raising her hand. Asa inclined her head, giving Jessamine permission to speak. "Miss, what about our plant? I know we will all take care of the village's plants, but what of our plant?" The other two, Cestrum and Hesna, nodded enthusiastically.

Asa sighed. One of the great Empress Horticulturist's first laws had been to create jobs for all fairies. This made sure that all plants would be healthy and safe. Infections would be taken care of before they became problems. That was why, in the village named Teasel Banksia, the six fairies that lived together all had specific jobs for maintaining harmony among the plants and themselves.

However, these three younglings seemed to think that they would only be caring for their mother plant. All three had been born from a Night Blooming Jasmine, and they were very protective of it. Well, Asa could understand that. Her own mother plant, a Ferula herb, held a special place in her heart.

However, she could not spend all of her time tending to the Ferula herb. In fact, most of her time was spent with a Scarlet Firebush that was going to give at least one new youngling.

She doubted it would give more than one, but that wasn't unusual. In fact, a situation like Jessa, Cestrum, and Hesna was far rarer. Three younglings from one plant. Anise, who had been caring for the plant at the time, definitely brought out the planet's potential.

"Your mother plant will be cared for by Anise and Cayenne, like she always is. You can check on her and bring her offerings, but you will care for the plants you are assigned to. Like the bahiagrass! It can always use another caretaker!" Asa explained as her patience wore thin.

Hesna raised her hand. Asa wearily gestured for her to speak. "Is it true that we could go to another village, somewhere other than Teasel Banksia, and work there?"

"Why would you want to leave mother!? Traitor!" Cestrum butted in.

Asa separated the bickering siblings. "Jessa, sit between them. Thank you. Yes, Hesna, it is true that you could relocate to another village. But you would have to go to the Cereus Palace first. It's important that we all are helping places that need the most help."

The younglings nodded. They understood that without them, Teasel Banksia might be one of those places that needed more help. They were the first younglings born in several years. The summer heat had dried up several mother plants, leading to the loss of many fairies. Asa was now the oldest fairy there, making her responsible for the health of the village.

Just as that thought crossed her mind, Elowenn, one of the strongest fairies of the village, came running up.

"Asa, come quickly. You need to see this!"

Chapter Three

Asa dismissed the children and followed Elowenn to her mother plant. It was a towering elm tree that shaded the entire village. Most of the fairies made their homes among the branches after leaving their mother plant. They all knew it well, but not as well as Elowenn. She was a guard and occasional messenger, unlike the rest of the fairies. Her mother tree was how she traveled and the source of her strength.

Asa knew that something had to be very wrong if Elowenn had come to her instead of dealing with the issue herself. Elowenn was a very resourceful fairy and one of Asa's finest pupils. She nervously fluttered after Elowenn, through the branches of the elm and up to the top. They paused on a twig, higher than Asa ever had reason to fly.

"I decided to check on the neighboring villages," Elowenn explained, "and I saw something strange. From the top of Mother, I can usually see the Magnolia Tree of Dionaea Muscipula and the Oak Tree of Euphorbia Obesa. But today, well... come look."

Asa followed Elowenn up above the elm and looked where Dionaea Muscipula was supposed to be. She saw nothing. That was the closest village, visible even from halfway up the tree trunk. Yet here, Asa couldn't see any trace that the village had existed.

Concerned, Asa spun around and looked for Euphorbia Obesa. The oak tree was there, but it was blackened, as if it had been badly burned. Wild fires weren't unusual, but the fairies never let them hurt the trees that much.

"What happened?" Asa asked, turning to face Elowenn. "Where are the fairies? How could this have happened?" Elowenn shrugged and motioned for Asa to follow her to the crook in the tree where she lived. The elm had mothered many fairies, but most had left to work in other villages. Elowenn, despite her youth, had the best branch to live on.

Elowenn's home was small but made of fresh young leaves. It was filled with the feathers of birds who shared the tree. The branches above had interwoven so tightly that rain never penetrated the shelter. Because it was near the trunk, the wind went around it, so Elowenn never had to replace anything in her house. Asa shook her head. The elm's youngling was spoiled by her mother.

Elowenn brought out a small shard of a rock. It reflected the light that hit it, scattering bright rainbows all around. The rock was translucent and had an orange tint. Asa could feel the power coming from it. Elowenn ran her fingers over the stone.

"It's a fire opal," she explained. "I found it under the oak this morning. I think, somehow, a fire opal was brought into the village and someone cracked it. It's the only thing that could create such a huge fire so fast."

"Where was it?" Asa asked, dreading the answer.

"Directly over the guardian plant."

Chapter Four

EVERY VILLAGE HAD A guardian plant. The guardian plant gave the village its name and the fairies their power. If the guardian plant of a village died, all of the village fairies would be weakened. Those who had been born from the guardian plant would perish. The plants around it, uncared for by the weakened fairies, would slowly wither and the whole village would die.

The guardian plant of Teasel Banksia lay safely surrounded by cacti and rose bushes. The village fairies alone knew the entrance to the plant. Visitors were forbidden from getting close enough to see it. The village of Euphorbia Obesa had its guardian plant safely tucked into the roots of the oak. The fairies had cultivated a strangler fig nearby to stand guard against those who wished it harm. Yet somehow, not only had a rare fire opal appeared near the plant, but it had shattered and released its power, destroying the whole village.

"Did you stop by Dionaea Muscipula as well?" Asa asked.

Elowenn nodded. "There's nothing there. The earth looks recently overturned. It's like the village was buried. Even the Magnolia Tree is gone. No trace of anything."

As the senior member of the village, Asa realized she had to take charge. "Well then, I will head to Cereus Palace to see if the counselors and ask for advice." After the passing of the Empress Horticulturist, the fairy community agreed to discontinue the tradition of Leading Horticulturists. This was due to the past troubles they had and the high standards Epazote III had set. So, the counselors made group decisions about everything that impacted the fairy community.

Elowenn nodded hesitantly. She supposed it was a good idea, but she was concerned about their strongest member leaving while villages around them were disappearing.

"How will you get there?" she asked. Typically, fairies made the trip by flying or on foot. Without villages to stop and rest at, going to the palace could take weeks. And that was only if the weather was favorable. During strong winds, fairies could be thrown back miles.

Asa smiled. She had a few tricks up her sleeve. After assuring Elowenn not to worry, she flew off to pack for her journey.

Chapter Five

ASA PACKED QUICKLY. SHE only brought one change of clothes, a canteen filled with a fresh dewdrops, and a pea. It would be enough to sustain her, at least until she reached another village.

She stepped outside and bumped into Elowenn. "I'm sorry, I'm really going to need an answer on how you're going to get there," Eloween said nervously. "I need to know if something goes wrong."

Asa laughed. "That's reasonable. Come with me. I'll show you!"

The older fairy headed to the Scarlet Firebush she cared for. She knelt beneath the plant and dug beneath the bud. When her hand brushed metal, she knew she had found what she was looking for. She pulled out a thin pipe made of sterling silver. Elowenn furrowed her brow when Asa put her lips to one end of the pipe and blew. A thin squeal sounded, and Asa pulled back, beaming. She gestured for Elowenn to follow her to the edge of the garden.

Elowenn was puzzled. She didn't understand how the whistle Asa had used would help get her to the palace any faster. Then a shadow fell over the two fairies. Elowenn looked up to see a huge mouth full of sharp teeth. She yelped in horror, glancing over at Asa who did not appear even mildly surprised. In fact, Asa looked quite pleased with the large animal's appearance, which seemed to be a dog.

"Asa," Elowenn murmured, "What, in the name of the firebush, is that...thing?!"

The older fairy laughed lightly. Asa flew up to pat the creature on its nose. It panted happily and lay down, which didn't change its height as much as Elowenn had hoped.

"This," Asa explained, tying her bag around the dog's neck, "is a corgi. Corgis are the best for long distances. They are made for carrying fairies and are incredibly smart. This particular corgi, Sir Cedric, will be taking me to the Cereus Palace."

The corgi barked in agreement. Elowenn shook her head and wished her elder luck.

Chapter Six

Asa mounted the corgi, gripping his fur tightly. She waved goodbye to Elowenn, who looked a bit ill. Then, digging her heels into Cedric's flanks, they took off.

Asa stopped Cedric when they reached what had been Dionaea Muscipula. Elowenn had been right. Asa couldn't see any sign of life, and the ground was freshly overturned. Cedric was very interested in the dirt. He pawed at one spot in particular.

Asa dismounted to look at what Cedric had found. He had unearthed something that was glittering in the dim light. The fairy picked it up carefully and gasped. It was a piece of a boulder opal. Not only that, but she was now sure that where she had been standing was where the guardian plant of the village had been. She remembered it well. The village hadn't even bothered to hide or protect it because it had been a glorious Venus Fly Trap. It devoured anything that neared it.

Asa realized this had been the downfall of the village. The boulder opal wasn't shattered like the fire opal had been, but the chemicals from the Fly Trap had dissolved the stone's edges. That must have released the power of the stone, causing the earth below to consume everything nearby. Asa shuddered. First fire, now earth.

She was seeing a pattern. She hoped she was wrong.

Asa climbed back onto Cedric and urged him on. He ran, and the world around her blurred from his speed. She loved riding corgis. They were so enthusiastic and capable, and they didn't tire easily. She knew Cedric could bring her to the Palace before he needed rest, which was good because the sun had just slipped below the horizon. It was dangerous to be traveling in the dark. Creatures like bats snacked on fairies.

It had only been ten minutes before Asa saw something strange in the distance. She knew she was passing a river soon and that there was a village near that river. But she heard a gurgle from the water, and it sounded almost aggressive. She turned Cedric toward the village, even though it was out of her way. She had a feeling something terrible was about to happen.

The river's gurgle became a growl. As Asa glanced upstream, she saw a rush of water pass over the bank. It was a flood!

Cedric saw this and refused to get closer to the river. Asa watched in horror as a wave crashed over the fairy village, sweeping away dozens of plants and fairies.

Chapter Seven

Asa and Cedric approached the remains of Typha, the flooded village. The river had carried away almost everything, including the guardian plant. Almost immediately after destroying the plants, the flood had subsided.

Asa spread her wings, which glowed slightly, and looked for what she knew had caused the rush of water. Cedric found it first. The black opal glistened in the shadows.

Asa swallowed nervously. She feared for her village and wondered what she would come across next. Briskly, she jumped onto Cedric and begged him to run faster than he had before. She knew her best hope would be the counselors. They would know what to do.

Asa was also grateful that there was no other villages separating them from the Cereus Palace. She was already feeling quite sad and couldn't bear to see more death.

Night fell, but Cedric had excellent vision in the dark. He ran powerfully into the shadows ahead without fear. Asa knew it wouldn't be a long trip at this speed, but she still found herself trembling.

Cedric woofed, and Asa glanced up. There was the Cereus Palace, glowing in the darkness from the wings of the guards and the power of the counselors. She let out a breath she didn't know she had been holding. The Cereus Palace was constructed from a hollowed out cactus, which was also its guardian plant. Cedric stopped in front of the Palace and allowed Asa to dismount before heading to the stables to eat and rest. Asa took a deep breath before entering.

The counselors had an open door policy. Asa explained all that she had seen, including the opals. She noted the worried looks on the three fairies' faces that sat before her, and then wondered why only three of the four counselors were in attendance.

Finally, Zemlja spoke. All of Asa's questions were answered, though her fears only grew. "This is very bad news, dearest. You see," the counselor said in a shaky voice, "Zrak, Fourth Counselor and Wielder of Air, has rebelled. He is seeking to destroy our world."

Chapter Eight

Asa understood everything too late. Zrak had rebelled. He had stolen all of the opals, aiming to destroy all fairies. Now he was breaking the gems in each village, releasing their power and ruining the guardian plants.

"He has already demolished villages elsewhere. There are only a few left. Serenoa Repens, Bambusoideae, Teasel Banksia, Schinus Terebinthifolia..." Vatra, another counselor, explained.

"But surely he has run out of opals by now. So my village is safe!" Asa exclaimed.

The counselors shifted uncomfortably. "He has run out of fire opals, boulder opals, and black opals," Voda agreed, "But we haven't heard of any cases with white opals yet. He has enough to take out the remaining villages with those."

Asa felt her heart sink. White opals... Surely the counselors could help save her village though. They wielded the elements. The elders looked even more uncomfortable when Asa mentioned this to them.

"We could...if he were using our elements. Now he is only using air, which he wields full control over. He was clever to use our opals before we understood what was happening. Unless he is caught, we cannot stop him," Vatra explained in a soft tone.

Asa couldn't believe what she was hearing. The most powerful beings in the fairy community were doing nothing to stop the destruction of their people. Not only that, but her village was in danger!

"If you won't help, fine. But I will not stay here while my village is destroyed by Zrak! I have three younglings there and one more yet to blossom! I must return!" With that, Asa turned on her heel and left the counselors.

She called out to Cedric. He pranced over, fearless and cheerful as ever. Leaping onto his back, they sped off. It was still dark, but dawn would come soon. The rising sun would bring danger to her village. She couldn't afford to wait until morning to return home.

She might already be too late.

Chapter Nine

THE SUN WAS STILL hidden when Asa saw Teasel Banksia. Sleepy fairies were tending to their plants and sipping dew, unaware of the danger they were in. Cedric was panting heavily as he ran toward the village, and Asa felt guilty for running him so much. However, she knew she had to hurry. Even if Zrak went for the other villages first, he appeared to travel fast.

Cedric dropped down at the Firebush, and Asa took off. She was met almost instantly by Elowenn, who had seen the corgi approaching from her spot on the elm.

"What have you learned?" Elowenn asked, but Asa cut her off, "No time, we must protect the guardian plant! Come quickly!" She flew past the Night Blooming Jasmine where the younglings were asleep in their buds and stopped their guardian plant.

The roses were bright red. The petals disguised the large thorns that shielded the guardian plant from intruders. Asa carefully pushed aside a petal from one of the larger flowers and inched into the maze of thorns. Elowenn followed her lead. Together they made their way past the roses and cacti to stand in front of their guardian plant.

So far, the plant was fine and showed no trace of intrusion. Asa inspected it carefully.

"I think it's safe," she concluded, satisfied. She heard a gasp from behind her and turned to see Elowenn looking at a spot above her. Following her gaze, Asa looked up into the wicked grin of Zrak.

The counselor was clutching a large white opal and had a glint of madness in his eyes. He had managed to squeeze between the thorns above the guardian plant. Asa realized he had sacrificed his wings to get there. The thorns had torn them to shreds, so he had lost all ability to fly. Yet he didn't seem to mind.

As Asa watched in horror, he lifted a twig with a particularly large thorn on it. She realized a second too late what his plan was. Zrak hit the shining surface of his opal with the thorn so hard that it scratched, and then he dropped the rock. Asa jumped up to try and stop it from hitting the guardian plant, but the wind that was released from the opal pushed her back. She was too late.

Chapter Ten

ASA MAY HAVE BEEN too late, but Elowenn wasn't. The younger fairy had launched herself at Zrak before he scratched the opal. She caught it in midair and zipped past Asa as fast as her wings could take her. Asa could hear the wind beginning to roar, but she couldn't worry about Elowenn now. She had Zrak to focus on.

Zrak scowled when his opal failed to blast open the guardian plant. He didn't waste time clawing his way out of the bushes. Asa took the longer but safer route out. Unfortunately, this put her several steps behind the Wielder of the Air, who couldn't fly with damaged wings but could run faster than Asa had ever seen a fairy run. The wind was howling intensely. Asa was forced to fold up her wings to keep from being blown away.

Zrak ripped a large leaf off of the nearest plant and held it above his head. Asa gasped when it lifted him into the air. He was getting away!

A vicious war cry let loose, and three fairies jumped out from the plant and grabbed Zrak's legs. Asa almost stopped in shock, but then she realized that Zrak hadn't ripped a leaf from just any plant... he had ripped one from the Night Blooming Jasmine. This had angered the plant's younglings.

Asa used a vine to bind Zrak and called to Cedric. "Take him to Cereus Palace and make sure he is given to the other counselors. They will take care of him," she ordered, and the corgi dipped his head to acknowledge her request.

Asa wasn't out of trouble yet. The wind was still shaking the elm tree, and she had to grab hold of the Jasmine to keep from blowing away. She scanned the sky for Elowenn.

She saw Anise instead. The other fairy was fighting the wind to get to her, shouting something repeatedly. Her voice kept getting lost in the wind, but Anise wasn't giving up.

Asa crept closer and grabbed Anise's arm to keep the fairy from flying off. "What were you saying?" Asa shouted over the loud wind.

"The Scarlet Firebush! She's blooming! A youngling is blossoming!"

Chapter Eleven

ASA KNEW THAT THE plants needed to be cared for during a blooming. She knew it was especially important if the wind was strong enough to rip a youngling from its blossom. She and Anise began to fight their way to the Firebush. It took several minutes, but they got there. Cayenne was holding the blossom still to keep the youngling safe.

"If it blooms in this wind, we won't be able to catch the youngling!" she shouted at Asa.

"We have to try!" Asa yelled back, as she took up a position next to her fellow fairy. They braced themselves. However, they didn't have to worry. As the flower unfolded, the wind stopped completely. The youngling fell onto the bahiagrass, unruffled and safe.

Asa helped the new fairy up. Younglings were unsteady on their legs for a few hours after blooming, and their wings would remain unopened for a few days. The new youngling would need support until she could stand on her own.

"Hello. My name is Hamelia, but you can call me Lia," the youngling peeped. She looked around, observing the fallen branches, torn leaves, and scattered fairies. Her brow furrowed, trying to understand the mess around her.

Anise started explaining things to Lia, and when she finished, she turned to Asa and asked what had happened to Elowenn.

Asa tried to process the question. She knew Elowenn had taken the opal away from the guardian plant. But she wasn't sure what happened to Elowenn after that. She knew the wind had stopped, but she didn't understand why. With all of the questions and everything that had been going on in the past few days, Asa fell onto the grass and passed out.

Chapter Twelve

Afterword

BECAUSE ZRAK HAD BEEN stripped of his title of counselor and wielder, a counselor position had opened up in the palace. Elowenn had taken Zrak's opal high in the air above an empty field and wrapped herself around it. The power from the opal flowed into her, and she suddenly found herself with a new position in the Cereus Palace. The other counselors welcomed Elowenn with open arms. Over time, they slowly replenished their supply of opals and put far greater security on the precious stones.

Asa, after coming to, was relieved to see that everything had been repaired. Lia adjusted well to life in Teasel Banksia. The three younglings cared for the elm in the absence of Elowenn. They were regarded as heroes due to the role they played in the capture of Zrak.

Anise was frazzled by the blossoming of so many younglings in the past month. She insisted on caring for the Ferula in the hope that she would not foster anymore blooms. Within a day, the Ferula had four buds forming. Cayenne promised to assist Anise as much as possible.

Sir Cedric had done such a fabulous job transporting fairies that he became an esteemed member of the Counselor Corgis and was pampered for the rest of his life.

Zrak was imprisoned in a dungeon room in Cereus Palace.

Without his power or his wings, his name was lost to history.

The villages that were demolished were restored by the counselors and several fairy survivors were found. After replanting and nurturing the guardian plants of the villages, the fairies regained strength. Over time, their villages flourished.

All was finally well again in the fairy world, and so it would remain for many years to come.

About the Author

Morgan Humphrey is a contributing author to the Storyshares library.

About the Publisher

Story Shares is a nonprofit focused on supporting the millions of teens and adults who struggle with reading by creating a new shelf in the library specifically for them. The ever-growing collection features content that is compelling and culturally relevant for teens and adults, yet still readable at a range of lower reading levels.

Story Shares generates content by engaging deeply with writers, bringing together a community to create this new kind of book. With more intriguing and approachable stories to choose from, the teens and adults who have fallen behind are improving their skills and beginning to discover the joy of reading. For more information, visit storyshares.org.

Easy to Read. Hard to Put Down.

Notes